Creepified

Creepified

Supernatual Beings

S.L. Armend

ReadersMagnet, LLC

1

While sitting in algebra class, my stomach started to rumble. Finally, the bell rang and it was time for lunch. Woo-hoo! Couldn't wait to sit down in the cafeteria to relax, enjoy, and share the midday meal with friends—if I had any friends.

Every day, in my last class, I could hardly wait for the last bell to ring so I could run home and hide in my room forever. Ever since I arrived at Reynolds Middle School last week, I've felt nothing but strange vibes and bad energy—at least that's what I thought it was.

How could I even begin to move up the social ladder at this school? Wearing cool clothes just wasn't cutting it. I couldn't show-off my awesome tennis skills on the court because this school had no tennis team or courts. I had to find another way to look cool and normal...pull myself up from the giant pit of losers that new kids usually get thrown into.

Shortly afterwards, while waiting for the *only friend* I had so far, Gordon Underwood, I planked my food tray down. He was still standing in the lunch line when I turned my head in time to see Danielle, Maya, and

Gina, walking in the cafeteria. I quickly turned the other way to avoid making any eye contact with them. The consensus around here was to hide from these girls—if you could. Or at least pretend not to see them.

But moments later…

"Oh…oh no!" some kid wailed.

I looked all around the cafeteria and realized what the boy was reacting to: He was soaking wet.

Danielle had dumped a soda on this poor guy's head. "So sorry, that was so clumsy of me," she said, holding back her laughter.

He put his head down and seemed to wince multiple times, but never uttered a word. Probably too embarrassed to come up with a clever retort. There was no doubt about it. Those girls were mean — mean at a DNA level.

"So, Dina Barro, what do you think about witches?" Gordon asked once he joined me for lunch.

"You mean aside from the fact that I don't believe in them? Not much, I guess."

"I totally believe in magic spells," Gordon said. "It's been well documented that they really do work."

"Documented where? *Spellbound Weekly Magazine*?" I laughed hysterically.

He squinted his eyes at me but kept talking. "They say that when a witch cuts hair off from you, she can use it to control you."

"That's hilarious," I rolled my eyes at him. "I guess I should run for my life as soon as I see someone holding a pair of scissors, ha?"

"How lame," he said. "Seriously. If they can't cut it with scissors, they'll find other ways…ways you can't even imagine."

"*What?!*"

Gordon just nodded. "In fact, some of the town's local witches are at our school."

"So, do they fly out of their houses on brooms," I laughed some more, "then park them at the bike rack when they get to school?"

Silence.

I didn't know how to stop. But I had to admit even I was getting tired of my own sarcasm.

"You're still new at this school," he grinned. "But around here, all this stuff I'm telling you is just common knowledge."

"Should I also be prepared to see pale, anemic adolescent vampires flying around our halls, too?" I covered my mouth with both hands, trying to look frightened. Trying.

"Don't be such a spaz, Dina. There are no pasty vampires lurking around these parts of the country," he shook his head. "We're just known for having witches—for now."

"And what about warts? You know, especially warts with hair growing out of them?"

"Nope. No wart-covered old hags in these areas or at our school," Gordon narrowed his eyebrows at me. "In fact, no modern-day witch fits that stereotype— and they're not green either."

This time I bit my lip. Gordon seemed to have piqued my curiosity. "So how did you guys find out they were witches?"

"One day, some girl went in the girl's restroom and the witches were chanting in the bathroom stalls—with the doors closed, of course," Gordon whispered.

"In the restroom?" I laughed. "But why in there?"

"Well, everyone thought it was some emergency chant right before semester finals...you know, so they could ace their exams...the bathroom was a better option than the hallways."

"So, what happened to the girl who walked in on them?" I demanded to know.

"She quickly walked out and waited around the hall until they were done," Gordon said as he lowered his voice even more. "She was able to identify them and rumors about their craft have been on overdrive since."

"Wow!" I said, leaning back on my seat. But this time, this time I was a bit more intrigued.

"Oh, and there was also the time when some kid followed them after school. The kid ended up deep in the forest with them, and then discovered their favorite place for worshiping."

"What did he see?"

"He told everyone the witches were sitting in a circle facing each other, that the light of several black candles and a smoldering, bubbling cauldron was able to cast a light on their faces."

"Did they see him?"

"Not right away. Apparently, the girls didn't even notice that he was standing a few yards away. They appeared to be in a *trance*."

"Then they caught him, right?" I asked excitedly.

"Well, sort of. Suddenly he was face-to-face with one of the girls…"

"OMG! Did she cast a spell on him, then?"

"No. He freaked out and asked her what she was doing there. Then she retorted, 'Isn't it obvious, *moron*? Besides, I should be asking *you* that!' And he dashed out of there."

"So, what happened?"

"The usual. He blabbed it to someone and eventually the whole school knew."

"Now everyone has seen them practicing their magic in the forest?" I asked, sounding genuinely interested this time.

He looked straight into my eyes. "I'd say almost all of the school have seen them by now."

When we finished eating, Gordon pointed out a couple of the school witches to me. I told him I wanted to befriend and get to know them.

Trying not to look so obvious, I slowly grabbed a chair and crammed myself in between two of them. "Hi girls, do you, um, mind if I join you for lunch today?"

They both looked at me like I was deranged. They shrugged their shoulders and nodded yes while continuing with their private chat. But even as I sat there, tightly packed, shoulder-to-shoulder with them, they continued to talk over my head. They kept passing each other stuff right in front of me as if I were just a backpack leaning on a chair. I felt awkward and as small and insignificant as a gnat.

So, I grabbed my milk carton and purposely started making loud, gulping sounds.

They rolled their eyes at me.

"*Sorrrreee!*" I said, lowering my head, now too embarrassed to ever look at them in the eyes again.

When I turned to look at Gordon, he just sat there shaking his head, looking as disappointed as I felt.

I couldn't figure out why was I suddenly drawn to the girls…those witches? It wasn't like anybody was daring me to befriend them. I had always been a nonbeliever in them and laughed at people who did believe in witchcraft. But now, an unexplainable force was pulling and pushing me towards them. Now that Gordon told me about them, I couldn't stop thinking of them. The more I tried to ignore what he told me, the more I wanted to know them.

The bell was about to ring and lunch would soon be over but I got nowhere with the two little witches. They never told me to get lost but they never included me in their conversation either. I had to think of another way to warm up to them and learn more about their *craft*. By now, I felt as if I was being left out of the adventure of a lifetime. Besides, what could go wrong by just watching these girls do a little magic? Everyone else had seen them. Why not me?

Then suddenly, Gordon grabbed my arm and pulled me to the side. "You know there's a rumor that

Mrs. Foster, an eighth grade English teacher, dabbles a little with witchcraft."

"Is she the one who goes crazy decorating her room for Halloween?"

"Yes," a grin broke across his face. "She's the one— She's no phony either; she sounds well-versed in that subject and its history—*she's authentic.*"

"What? Even teachers are witches here?" I exclaimed. "What kind of school is this? The American version of *Hogwarts School of Wizardry?*"

"That would be so cool!" he beamed.

I smiled back even though I kept telling myself over and over that there was no such thing as witches, witchcraft, and magic. Period."

"Well, there's more. Last year one of her students," Gordon continued, "claimed she saw a ghost of a girl in Mrs. Foster's classroom closet."

"What? Spooks, too?"

"Yes. She tells her students that the ghost has been hanging around in her closet since she started teaching here."

"Did the dead girl speak to the student?"

"No. There was never an exchange of words between them. She communicates occasionally with the teacher only."

"But that's crazy." I raised my hands up. "What does Mrs. Foster say about all that?"

"She tells everyone that the spirit is simply stuck. You know, like not able to continue her journey to *the other side.*"

"Because of unresolved issues and business in the physical world, right?" I blurted out.

"Nope. The apparition told the teacher she's just afraid of what lies ahead for her."

"But—why?" I implored.

"Because she was a chronic prankster up until the day she died…she's afraid she'll pay for it by burning in the fires of you-know-where."

"Yikes! So, she probably died playing a dangerous prank on someone, ha?"

"Yep," Gordon nodded. "A practical joke gone bad."

"But what was the prank?"

"Who knows. The girl has always refused to tell the teacher."

My mouth was slowly forming a big, long O of surprise.

"Anyway, Mrs. Foster told the student that her classroom ghost has continued to hang around there because she is attracted to the energy there. Her need to be in that location is really strong."

"Do you think this was the place where she met her untimely death?" I shrilled.

"The teacher believes that might be the case—probably before this school was even built," Gordon said. "Even though that's something the *lost soul* won't reveal to her, she strongly senses it."

"Hmmmm. I'd like to see that classroom and its closet," I said, squinting my eyes and rubbing my chin.

"I can introduce you to the teacher today, after school, if you'd like."

"Yeah, do that!" I agreed without hesitation.

Of course, it was my nature to be skeptic about this sort of stuff, but I still couldn't wait to meet Mrs. Foster—and hopefully, her little phantom friend, too.

2

After our last class, I scrammed down the hall to meet Gordon in front of the haunted classroom. Before either one of us could knock, the door began to open slowly. It cracked and creaked like an old tree on a windy day.

"Come right in, guys," Mrs. Foster hollered as she erased an assignment off the board. "I've been expecting you."

The very popular teacher was a little chubby, with reddish-brown frizzy hair just past her shoulders. Her skirts were ankle-length with that wrinkly, gauzy fabric look. Her blouse was long sleeved, flowy, airy-looking—like a hippie from the 1960s.

Gordon and I exchanged glances and smiled as we slowly walked towards her. She finally stopped cleaning the board and turned to us gleaming warmly. "Hello Gordon. Dina. You're here about the once mischievous child who's now a ghost, ha?"

My eyes opened wide and my skin prickled with excitement and fear. "Wow, you do have magical and psychic powers," I wrapped my arms around myself.

"Well, yes, except for the part about why you are here," she said, laughing and throwing her head back. "Most kids come to see me about the classroom spirit."

"Wow, what eeriness. What spookiness. I love it!" I cried. "Can we see her? Can we see her now?"

Mrs. Foster held her finger in front of her mouth, signaling me to be quiet. "She tends to be shy around new students," she whispered.

Seriously? A sensitive and bashful ghost? I mumbled, turning to look at Gordon. Then as she walked to show us the closet, an unexplainable force seemed to propel my feet towards the closet, beating her to the door.

Gordon just stood there, shaking his head. "Aren't you the tiniest bit scared of her?"

"No. How silly," I retorted, swinging the door wide open. But as usual, I acted in a hasty manner.

"Look! Look!" Gordon pointed to the middle of the closet.

"Huh?" I breathed a mixture of exhilaration and horror. Then our eyes bugged-out and our jaws dropped down to our knees.

Right before us, papers…dozens of white, printer paper…were swirling around like a twister ready to cause extensive damage.

"Stand back!" Mrs. Foster ordered. "She might be feeling a little overwhelmed about—you know——the stream of ongoing kids wanting to meet her this year."

Gordon and I stood motionless. Frozen. Too afraid to even breathe.

But the girl's ghost never materialized to any of us — only her whirling, mass of energy filled with angst.

Then suddenly the closet door slammed shut! I took a deep breath, another step back, and started blinking uncontrollably.

"Listen kids, don't come unglued," Mrs. Foster warned, "but it's best we cut this visit short and leave the classroom immediately—sorry."

We both gasped at the same time.

"Let's go," Gordon pleaded as he dug his short nails into my arm. We quickly said good-bye to Mrs. Foster and zoomed out of her room.

"Wow, I really liked her," I said, letting out a great big sigh. "I want to be just like her when I grow-up."

"An English teacher?" Gordon asked.

"No. A psychic and a witch!"

Gordon just shook his head and rolled his eyes.

"Hey, I never asked her about witchcraft!"

"Some other time, Dina—when *ghost-girl* is in a better mood!"

Then as I walked home, it occurred to me, for someone that had always laughed at, and made fun of all things *supernatural*, I was now feeling a wave of bone-chilling goosebumps throughout my whole body.

3

The next day, when I got to my locker, through my peripheral vision, I could see Danielle and her *click* strutting down the hall, side-by-side. Everyone was frantically trying to clear the path for the school's three princesses to pass and get through.

Once they stopped at their lockers, they shamelessly started flirting with Dominic Palma who was passing by with his girlfriend.

Well, obviously, his girl wasn't too happy about that and the couple got into a shouting match over that. The girlfriend stormed off and left him standing in the hallway, scratching his head.

Oh, but they weren't done yet. Danielle spotted me at my locker…caught me looking right at her. There was no time to run for my life—or pretend I didn't see her. Danielle whispered something to the girls and they headed right towards me. She grabbed my locker door and slammed it shut. My heart started racing and my hands were shaking.

"Later, kid," she said, tossing her wavy, blond hair back.

All three of them howled with laughter as if they had just done or said something hilariously funny and witty. Then they walked away, shaking their heads, pumping their fists in the air. I guess if their purpose in life was to spread misery, they were doing a very good job at it.

After school, I told Gordon I wanted proof that these girls practiced witchcraft. I insisted he take me and show me where they performed their ceremonies. "Go ahead, make a believer out of me!" I gave him a cold, hard stare. "I dare you."

"It could work," he said, rubbing his chin. "It definitely could work."

"What do you mean? What could work?"

"Taking you there so you can see for yourself, of course!" he grinned mischievously.

We slapped each other a high five.

"Prepare to be amazed!" Gordon said as we walked home in opposite directions.

That night, I couldn't fall asleep. I kept twisting, turning, and squirming under my covers. All I could do was think about spying on the witches and maybe… eventually becoming their friend.

I tried everything from counting backwards to counting everything in my room. But I was wide awake. There were too many thoughts swirling around my head — too many crazy ideas—ideas about *the world of magic*.

The following morning, I was feeling uneasy about my first period class, biology. I wasn't looking forward to dissecting a frog that day because of my love for all animals, especially if they ended up dead for lab work. The second reason, well, that was simply the *yuck* factor. But there was no way around this. There weren't any other options like extra credit to replace it.

Okay, I lied. There was the computer-based-model choice—but everyone would think I was a big baby if I went that route.

Oh, and another reason I was feeling troubled — Danielle was in my class, too. Since our little encounter at my locker, she was going to be harder to ignore now. But hey, at least I didn't have to pair-up with the bully while trying to cut open a slimy frog.

Standing next to me was my dissecting buddy, Serena Massey. She had long, brown hair down to her knees, which swayed from side-to-side when she walked down the halls. Her facial features were fine and delicate and every time she smiled, two great, deep dimples would appear.

"I'll help you get over the *squeamishness* if you help me too," she smiled. "Together we can make it through this middle school rite of passage."

All I could do was give her half a smile. Then we both put on our black smocks, plastic goggles, and rubber gloves.

"Should be interesting opening up this poor formaldehyde-drenched frog just to pick at its insides," I said, cringing.

"Remember, it will still emit a pungent odor and still be slimy," she reminded me.

"Ugh—like I'm not already seriously grossed out," I rolled my eyes.

A half hour later, we had successfully cut open our little frog without throwing up or fainting.

Then out of the corner of my eye, I saw something flying across the classroom and headed towards the windows.

Correction. It was headed straight at me. "Ribbit… ribbit," it greeted me. A *live* frog had just landed next to the tray—the dead frog's tray—where it was pinned down. As you can imagine, things got messy. Serena and I were startled. I spilled the pins all over the floor, the dissecting tray spun around, and the scalpel flew out of Serena's hand.

"AAAAAAA!" I screamed.

"Hey!" Serena yelped. "Who brought the live frog to class?"

The whole class started laughing. I could now feel perspiration beads oozing through my pores and forming on my forehead.

"Did you girls bring that frog to class?" Mr. Parker, our biology teacher asked, sounding irritated.

"No, we didn't!" we both answered in unison, our voices shaking.

"Um, Mr. Parker, sir," I said nervously, "didn't you see that it was thrown at us?"

His eyes grew wide. "Sorry, I was busy filing papers—but someone in this classroom brought that frog."

"This morning, I heard someone say they brought a frog to school to play jokes on people," Danielle said. "Maybe it was left in this classroom on purpose."

I turned around to look at her, and sure enough, she flashed me a diabolical grin as she twirled her blonde hair.

She was guilty, all right.

But I was starting to worry now. I didn't know how much more of them I could tolerate before they finally left me alone—if ever! Would I ever stand up for myself? The ongoing moments of constant humiliation and ridicule these girls endlessly caused everybody around here had been slowly damaging my psyche for some time now.

It was time for me to FIGHT BACK!

I knew now that I had to stand up to Danielle, Maya, and Gina. I wasn't just getting tired of them; I wanted them to *fear and respect me*, too!

"Don't fret," Gordon said as we walked home. "You'll find a way to get those girls off your back. Once you've been here for a while, they'll get tired of picking on you."

"Are you kidding?" I snapped. "I'll be old and gray before they stop tormenting me. Transferring out of here is probably my best option."

"Hmmm, too bad you can't cast a spell on them to leave you alone," he laughed.

I shook my head. "You really do believe in witchcraft, don't you?"

"Sure, I told you I did. I also believe in monsters and UFOs."

"Well, I'm not sure I would ever be brave enough to get into witchcraft. I'd rather not mess with that sort of stuff. Really. I'm in enough trouble with the school bullies as it is."

"Yeah, I know. I was just kidding," Gordon said.

But I was so preoccupied about my life at that moment, I didn't even answer him. I was trying so hard to think of a plan and a way to handle my predicament with those girls that my brain felt as if it were spinning right out of my skull. The thought of not returning to school at all…EVER entered my mind…you know, like dropping out. Of course, that would create a much worse problem—my parents would freak out. They would ground me until I turned 30—maybe even for life!

4

The next day was Friday, teachers' conference day. We were let out early from school and I finally convinced Gordon to take me to the forest.

"Dina, tell me this," Gordon demanded trying to catch his breath. "How did I let you talk me into this—especially after you just told me yesterday that you didn't want to mess with any of them?"

"Because I'm your new *BFF*," I teased, catching up to him. "Besides, all I want to do is watch them — just spy on them a little."

Gordon was already a few yards ahead of me when I finally snapped out of it and focused on my surroundings. There was a wickedly windy sound that was beginning to flow through the trees. I stumbled my way through the dense foliage that kept blocking most of the sunlight. At times, I blindly stretched out my hands and had to feel my way through. I knew we were doomed and outnumbered as I fought a curtain of forest.

Then we could hear a girl's voice, high and excited, rising-up from somewhere nearby, and we suddenly stopped as we tried to make out the strange words she spoke. They were unusual but poetic. A minute later, several other voices joined in and started reciting the same words.

"Is that them?" I asked.

Without even answering, Gordon headed in the direction of the voices. It was getting easier to find them because the girls were now chanting at the top of their lungs. Then, there they were. Cassandra held the spell book up close to her face as she chanted, gliding her fingers over the words.

I could tell that Gordon was totally captivated by the blank expression on his face.

We both stood there numb for a while, neither one of us moving a muscle, watching the girls in their long, flowy gowns. Watching. Watching.

"Nothing's happening. Their chant—it hasn't worked," I said, sounding anxious.

And then we saw little balls of soft lights floating randomly above their heads. Cassandra stood motionless, gripping the spell book with both hands. She stared in amazement, shaking her head, appearing proud of her triumph. The other girls were rolling their heads delicately, stretching out their arms as if trying to reach for the illuminated bouncing spheres.

"Now do you believe?" Gordon complained, pointing at the coven. "You just wouldn't accept anything I said as the truth unless you saw it with your very own eyes. So, there you are."

"I get it. You weren't just teasing me because I'm the new kid in school."

Gordon crossed his arms and shook his head. "They not only practice magic, but their powers are supposed to increase with every full moon, too."

"So, if we come back and watch them in one month, their performance will be even greater?"

"Yes! That's why the cycles of the moon are so important to them."

"Hmmm. From now on, I'm going to make sure I mark those dates down on my phone's calendar."

Gordon suddenly yanked me down, lowering me closer to the ground. "They say that during their ceremonies, when they commune with nature and the universe, the forest starts to crawl with supernatural beings."

"Well, you're just a walking encyclopedia when it comes to this subject, aren't you?" I said between giggles. "Are you sure you're not one of them?"

"Nah, I'm not into that sort of stuff," he said with a stoic look on his face. "I just like being informed."

"Oh, wow," I murmured, narrowing my eyebrows. "What are those tiny lights circling around them now? They kind of look like glowing moths."

"Well, like I just said, supernatural beings. Those are fairies and sprites. Cassandra conjures them up every time she recites an incantation."

"Well, I've always known about fairies, but what are sprites?"

"They're like fairies," Gordon informed me. "They can be helpful, but they can also be hostile and harmful beings."

"So, are they *fairy wannabes?*"

"I wouldn't say that because they're more like tree spirits, ghost like."

"Yes, but can they hurt us?" I demanded.

Gordon cleared his throat. "Uhmm, they're mostly harmless…unless they feel threatened…if someone upsets them, they can be dangerous—unintentionally, though."

"Great!" I tightened my mouth. "Temperamental, supernatural creatures."

"Rumor has it they were all pretty frightened when these little beings suddenly appeared one day," Gordon continued. "Especially the newer girls who had just joined the coven. They all begged Cassandra to send them back where they came from."

"Did she?"

"Yes. She put them back in their appropriate element. But later, they learned more about them and how to treat them. Now, it seems they call upon them and want them around all the time."

I took a deep breath and turned toward their circle of magic. "If they continue to practice the craft," Gordon added, "it seems everything will always go their way; they will never have to worry about things the rest of us worry about…"

"Hmmm, I thought they had it all because they were just spoiled, rich girls."

"Dina, everyone at school tries to keep them happy. They've been doing everything they can to keep those girls from getting angry—just in case they should decide to retaliate against someone and cast a spell on them."

I just kept shaking my head. "They're that afraid of them?"

"Heck yeah! Most kids think the girls will chant a spell right in front of them, straight out of the book, and turn them into a big, fat TOAD!" He swallowed hard.

"So they are feared and untouchable by all. How cool is that?"

"Dina, this is crazy," Gordon whispered. "We need to leave now? Let's just get out of here!"

"But I want to see more," I insisted.

"This is way better than a movie."

"Ugh. Okay, so you've now seen their domain," he snapped. "This is where they come to reinforce their magical powers, commune with nature, fairies, furry animals, and feathered ones too." He gestured to the woods around as hidden creatures scuttled through the shrubbery that surrounded us. "Now let's leave before we get caught."

In all honesty, though, part of me did agree with Gordon. Sneaking around in the forest to spy on the school witches was probably a bad idea. But there we were, the two of us, hiding behind thick trees and bushes, our eyes fixated on the girls as they stood around in a circle holding hands.

"Weird. They're wearing what looks like ivory long gowns with flowy wide sleeves," I said, changing the subject. "Check out their cool-looking gold, cord belts."

"But look at Cassandra, the head witch," Gordon nudged me. "She's sporting a dark-purple, hooded robe. I hear that color symbolizes her great knowledge and experience of the craft."

"What is that weird smell?" I complained.

"They're probably burning incense and cooking special herbs and powders in that cast-iron, three-legged cauldron."

I pointed my nose up into the air, scrunching and twitching it. "Hmmmm…the smell kind of grows on you. Don't you think?"

"Not so much," he frowned. "They're probably preparing a witch's brew and potions—you know, stuff to go along with their spells."

And then I could see a faint smoke rising from their black mini-cauldron. Cassandra began to light candles. They seemed to be mounted on a makeshift altar.

"Listen!" Gordon exclaimed. "They've started chanting something different. And get a load of how their flowy-wide sleeves look like wings as they open their arms."

"Hey, maybe they fly around on that frail-looking broom by the tree?"

"Not a chance."

"Why not?"

"Contrary to popular belief, the broom-like thing is used to sweep an area of negative energy right before a ritual—like the one we're looking at now—it's just a symbolic tool," Gordon said sounding knowledgeable as usual.

"Wait, don't tell me, Mrs. Foster the English teacher told you that, right?"

"Of course, she's the expert on that subject."

"So, I take it their skin won't turn green and warty as they get older either, ha?"

I could see Gordon trying to control his laughter by covering his mouth with one hand and placing the other on his stomach. "That's so Hollywood, Dina. Trust me, floating a few feet above ground is as close to flying as they'll ever get—which is still quite supernatural and super cool, if you ask me."

"Okay, I've already told you I'm not feeling too good about this anymore," I choked. "What if they see us and come after us? What if they cast a spell on us? What if..."

Gordon grabbed me by my shoulders and spun me around to face him. "What if you had just listened to me in the first place, ha?"

Then we both froze. Gordon was breathless, stumbling over some bushes. He stared at me, his mouth open.

I had to keep rubbing my eyes. "What the..."

Then we both let out short cries as we were suddenly surrounded by some of the tiniest, delicately winged, and illuminated beings I had ever seen—real fairies and sprites!

Startled and spooked, I took several steps back.

"No-no!" Gordon sputtered. He pointed a now trembling finger at the little, flying things. "We're—we're busted! These pesky, airborne menaces are very protective of the girls and will rat on us for sure!"

One dove straight to my head. As I started to shriek, I became frantic and accidently swatted at it with the back of my hand. Several more speeding critters aggressively came at me. Their small, tiny hands yanked at my hair, like our thorny bushes back home. They gathered around me as if taunting me while they continued to whirl faster and faster.

The more I ducked my head and squatted down, the more they spun like twirling tops around me. They made a buzzing sound, too, like bees. Then again,

I inadvertently swung my hand and knocked-out another one. I saw it fall in some bushes.

Gordon grabbed my arm and dug his neatly trimmed nails into my flesh. His eyes went wide, and he opened his mouth in a high shriek of terror.

"I killed them!" I cried uncontrollably. "I just murdered two fairies—or at least given them some serious brain damage!"

He turned to me, his features tight with fear. "We're in big—I mean, *you're in big trouble now.*"

Then the first tiny, dainty-winged creature I hit reappeared and was suddenly giving me a very sinister stare. Before I knew it, it raged at me like an angry bull flaring its nostrils, head-butting me and even scratching me with its wee, microscopic fingernails. A throbbing pain then followed this.

I could see Gordon breathing hard as he tried to hide. "I told you they were known for getting even and could be dangerous if treated badly!"

They continued to annoy us by zooming around us like vicious, blood-thirsty parasites.

"We've got to get out of here and lose them!" I exclaimed. I started running back the same path we were on earlier.

Gordon bolted out of there too. "I'm not coming back here any time soon," he wailed, pushing frantically through bushes, shrubs, and trees.

I guess I must have been allergic to fairies, because my eyes were suddenly getting watery. The more I wiped them to try and clear them, the more I saw shimmering blurs of grays and blacks.

"Did they follow us?" I asked gasping for air.

"I—I'm not sure!" Gordon stammered, looking around for them. "But remember, they're supposed to get bored and leave people alone once they're ignored. I think we just accomplished that."

"Ow!" I shouted out as I stumbled over an exposed and protruding tree root.

Gordon, right behind me, nearly toppled over me. He reached down and helped me up. I had slightly twisted my ankle and was now in pain— but too afraid to stop running.

But hey, the mischievous fairies and sprites were gone!

We finally reached the roadside and headed toward my house, too freaked-out to exchange any words. We just kept running. But before arriving home, there was a small patch of woods we still needed to contend with. There we were, blindly ducking low branches and sliding on muddy spots like an endless nightmare.

At one point, I stumbled and staggered forward. But we finally reached my house, gasping for air. As we burst inside through the kitchen door, I peeked quickly through the window. I was relieved to see no sign of the woodland creatures. Maybe they weren't allowed to fly beyond their natural habitat: the forest.

Gordon and I sped up the stairs, down the hall and into my room. He was still struggling to breathe normally. I had another impulse to look out a window again. Good. Still no sign of them. Meanwhile, Gordon gently took off his sneakers and carefully scraped off the mud over my trash can. I just took mine off and tossed them in my closet. We hung out until dinner and then his mother picked him up.

I really thought Gordon was making this fairy and sprite stuff up. I was sure that anything that dainty and diminutive had to be harmless—but I was wrong. After that day, I knew they were trouble.

Later that evening, I wanted to relax and not worry about anything with wings, but my brain kept telling me not to get too cozy—yet.

The best I could do for now was lean back on my headboard, put my headphones on, and listen to some music.

Well, I must have dozed-off because as I slowly opened my eyes, I realized I wasn't alone. The fairy I hit was not only in my room, but was now sitting on the palm of my trembling hand. She shook. I stared at her and she yawned. Then my eyes shifted up to its tiny, little hand that was holding tightly to an even tinier magic wand.

I wanted to lock her up in my dirty clothes hamper. Instead, I raised it…brought it closer to my face. My hand just kept bringing her closer and closer—as if some powerful force was commanding me to do so.

Gaze at her, something kept telling me. *Gaze at her*.

I could hear her itty-bitty whisper inside my head. Was the teensy, weensy thing communicating with me? Was she trying to hypnotize me with her magical powers…eventually controlling my mind forever?

It seemed like her adrenaline must have kicked in because she started flying erratically like an annoying fly in a room searching for food and a place to land on.

Then when I saw her coming straight at me, I dropped to my stomach and once again started flapping my arms all over the place. At times my hand was open, but then at times I was punching my fist into the air. All I knew was that I was in survival mode.

Suddenly, it occurred to me to try to grab her delicate wings. Missed. Grabbed again.

Yes! I finally had her left wing pinched between my fingers. It felt silky-soft. I squeezed it gently, praying that I wouldn't tear it. And carefully, I lifted her up to my face. With my free hand, I covered my mouth.

I was shocked to see a pair of tiny, little eyes staring right at me. They were a piercing, deep-green, with even tinier, curly lashes. Before I knew it, this tiny creature had me in a hypnotic trance.

Then the mystic being's arms reached forward, menacingly, as if trying to grab me. But she didn't. Instead, she shook herself rigorously, as super-fine fairy dust fell from her sleeves and wings. What she caught in her hands, she slung at me. It shimmered like gold, then changed to colors of pink, purple, and silver. I sneezed.

Then I could see her itty-bitty lips move. I couldn't make out what she was saying; I could only hear a teensy-weensy, high-pitched, buzzing sound. Then pointing her little wand at me, she began to raise me to the ceiling and spin me around like a funnel of dried-up leaves. At that moment, I knew that she had been able to levitate me with the help of her magic powder. Then like a boulder, I hit the floor, followed by more sneezing. Everything about the fairy might have been tiny and cute, but as I lay there on the floor, I started hearing an evil, maniacal laugh. If you heard it, you'd think it was bone-chilling.

But then she stopped. And when I looked up, she was gone. Probably flew right through my opened window. I shut it immediately!

The next morning, when I walked into my bathroom, the little menace with wings had emptied my mouthwash bottle and filled it with cotton balls. Not fully awake, it took me approximately five minutes to realize no liquid would be coming out any time soon. Then when I reached for my acne face cleanser, you'll never guess what came out. Yes, mouthwash. I took a handful of the stuff and like an idiot, splashed my face, and started rubbing it in…but generated no lather…just minty skin.

Did I scream? Of course. You would, too, if a bothersome, little-winged supernatural being was now annoying you more than the mean girl at school. Suddenly, she zoomed right by me, so close she tickled my nose. I sneezed. Then I could hear her wickedly laughing all the way back to my bedroom.

I went after her. My eyes shifted left, right, up, and down, but she had vanished. Then I felt a gentle tug at my belt. Before I knew it, the little tug soon turned into a sudden twirl. It made me dizzy, causing me to stumble and almost fall.

After my light-headedness subsided, I looked down at my pant pocket and shrieked. The airborne bully wasn't finished with me. There she was, poking out of my pocket like some McDonald's Happy Meal *toy*. Grinning, too.

Petrified with fear, I wondered how else she would be taking revenge on me for slapping her. I worried this could be on ongoing battle because, after all, I was just a mere mortal and could never beat the powers of any supernatural being.

Then she started wiggling her way out of my pocket, opened my window, and flew out gracefully. I watched as she drifted through our back-yard jungle. Then she slipped into a mist of fine, sparkly dust and vanished.

"Oh, wow. Why would she suddenly stop picking on me?"

Not that I was complaining, but her sudden departure was just so weird.

I blinked hard, trying to make sure I wasn't just seeing things. But it appeared she was really gone. Flew back to her world of enchantment. Never to return? I could only hope.

At lunch, I told Gordon all about my fairy adventure at home. How lucky I was to have been stalked and followed by the vindictive creature all the way into my room.

"What? And you didn't text me about it?" He bellowed.

"Give me a break!" I exclaimed. "I was super freaked-out about it! It was an extraordinary circumstance that crippled my body and mind."

"You know, I really regret my involvement in the events that finally led you to this mess," he admitted. "I should've kept my mouth shut about all this witch stuff."

"Uh huh. Listen, I appreciate your brutal honesty, Gordon, but I would've found out about them through someone else in school, anyway."

"Yeah, but I took you to the forest and everything."

"I would've convinced someone else to take me there, too. Relax, dude." Suddenly I grabbed Gordon's arm. "Did you just see Danielle's eyes?"

Gordon cleared his throat. "I would say they're a little less beady today."

"But still up to something…she's always up to something," I kept nodding my head. Then I got a wave of anxiety that I just couldn't shake off.

"Can't we just focus on our lunch and pretend she doesn't exist," he said, optimistically naïve."

"Wait, what?" Seriously?" I rolled my eyes.

"You have to admit, there are lot more scarier things in this world than, Danielle."

"But they don't keep coming back like a pesky skin infection, do they?" I snapped.

By now, Gordon's mouth was so grossly stuffed with food that all he could do was shrug his shoulders.

I turned to him again. "I swear, if they sit anywhere near us, I'm moving to another table!" But when I turned back to look at them, they were gone. I turned to my left. Right. Stretched my neck over people's head. They were nowhere to be seen.

Gordon pulled his chair closer to me. "C'mon girl, get a grip. You're falling apart on me here!"

"Yeah, sorry. You're right." I frowned staring off into space. "There's no point in living in constant fear of them." Then suddenly, I started feeling pumped and psyched. A sense of fearlessness began to flutter and swirl inside me. It seemed to be gaining strength and momentum, until— "AAAAAAAAAAAAA!" I sat up, screaming so hard I felt my tonsils throbbing and pulsating.

Gordon looked startled, his eyes got big and round like saucers.

Fearing the worst, I closed my eyes tightly, slowly reached to touch the back of my legs. NIGHTMARE!

My jeans were soaked.

Gordon gulped hard, practically choking. "Did you just wet...?"

"Of course not, doofus!" I roared. "What's wrong with you?"

When I opened my eyes, the whole cafeteria was watching me. Shocker, ha? I wanted to crawl into a dark abyss of a crater and never be seen again. But all I could do was bite my lips as everyone started laughing at me.

Scrambling to the girl's bathroom, I caught Danielle, Maya, and Gina peeking through the cafeteria's side glass door. As they peered at me mischievously, they started giggling like infantile brats. OMG, it was them. How they did it, I wasn't sure...but they were guilty... they had done it to me again!

For a while, I stood staring at the mirror in the bathroom, counting the water droplets splashed all over the sink counter. I was feeling just as small and insignificant as those water drops. My tolerance for humiliation had finally maxed-out and I was thinking of calling in sick tomorrow. But what would I use as an excuse for the next day? And the next?

Well, after being excused early from school, for obvious reasons, I sent Gordon a text to meet me at my house after school.

"What? You want to join the witches' coven?"

"Sure, why not?" I said, sounding whimsical. "I may even be a lone witch."

"Well, don't be fooled," he warned. "The world of magic is not as idyllic as it looks."

"Okay, I confess that I've been often-times conflicted about taking this step, but I'm a pretty level-headed girl," I turned my nose up to the air. "So, no worries, everything should be cool."

"I thought their practice of the craft alone disqualified them as potential friends for you." Gordon sounded confused. "Weren't you the one that said all witchcraft was a hoax?"

"That was before I became fed-up with the wicked adolescents at school," I answered angrily. "Besides, Cassandra and the girls are more about good and kindness—you know, white magic."

"I just assumed you thought they were a bunch of freaks—that they ought to fly far away on their broomsticks?"

"Yes, I admit I thought that about them. But I guess I'm an expert at irony—besides, I just want see what I can do to make them leave me alone...so that they don't bully anyone else either."

"Dina, please listen to me. If you decide to get carried away with magic, it can have disastrous consequences," he implored, "but more importantly, it can have eternal consequences for your immortal soul. What do you think of that, ha?"

"Dude, you're always so dramatic."

"Well, don't come crying to me when you suddenly become nothing but a puddle of liquid on the floor—crying to be changed back to human form!"

"Listen, I'll just ask Cassandra to help me get Danielle off my back...the right way...in a kindly manner."

"Well, the girls really do know their craft." Gordon finally agreed, changing his tone. "But that's only if you become their apprentice and take their suggestions."

"I think I'll go as a witch for Halloween this year," I suddenly blurted out.

"So, no costume this year, eh?"

"Clever...hahaha...so clever," I said as I pushed him out the front door.

After Gordon went home, I lay on my bed, pondering the huge step I was about to take.

I couldn't help myself. I was dying to go back to the woods and spy on our little witches again. I already knew how to get there — the best spot to hide from them. This time, I was even planning to record it all on my phone before building enough courage to approach them.

Deep inside, I realized a lot of things about magic spells and incantations could make my heart skip a beat. Heck, sometimes just watching movies about this sort of stuff could have me jumping out of my skin. But hey, I wasn't a kid anymore; I was almost thirteen. What was I afraid of?

Sure, now that I had witnessed real magic, my instincts were now telling me I should never play around with this sort of stuff — that I could mess up a spell and conjure-up who knows what kind of evil entity. But I was fed up with being ridiculed and tormented daily at school even more. And enough was enough. No more being a wimp and a fraidy-cat. That day, was the day I was no longer going to let my crisis crush me—I was now going to allow it to transform me—and soon I would be embracing a brand-new me.

Well, that day finally arrived. I could almost feel their spell book in my hands. All its contents would be my daily supplement for bravery and retaliation. I would use it each day until I could get even with Danielle and her BFFs.

Sweet. I would soon rise above them—not only figuratively, but maybe even literally.

Once I reached the edge of the forest by the roadside, I looked up at the tall trees. I hesitated at the thought of walking into the dark, shadowy parts in the distance. It was still and quiet except for the sounds of birds above, squirrels, and rustling of other animals on the ground.

I could feel the difference in temperature as I walked in from the sunny roadside to the cool shade of nature's umbrella. There were sections where the sky and sun rays managed to peer through, like spotlights on someone performing on stage. The ground appeared damp with some grassy patches here and there. Then like a klutz, I stepped on what I knew for sure was some animal dropping.

"Yuck!" I squealed. "That's disgusting!"

I could hear some commotion ahead.

I continued to follow a narrow path that sometimes curved and twisted.

Then I suddenly tripped and fell to my knees and tore some moss off a tree's exposed root. It had an earthy smell to it and felt soft and damp.

"Oh, wow. Nice start. Just got here and already had two mishaps." It almost felt as if someone or something was trying to tell me to turn around and go back home.

Well, I started toward the trail again, but about five minutes later, my left shoe began to sink into some soft soil. "Whoa!" I let out a frightening moan. I was now struggling to lift my foot out of some of the gooiest mud ever—or, maybe it was dangerous quick sand! "Oh, what next?" I yelled out.

By now, there was no doubt in my mind that the universe was trying to tell me something. Every time I fell and stumbled, it felt like a sign and warning not to continue my journey through the woods.

Then a creepy, bone-chilling feeling came over me. You know, the kind you get when somebody is watching you…like spooky eyes gazing upon you from the deep darkness.

"I'm not afraid to be here!" I hollered as I frantically tried removing the mud off my shoe with a piece of tree branch. "You don't scare me!"

Dozens of birds suddenly flew out of trees, followed by the scurry of little feet on the damp ground below.

I stood still, listening hard, expecting a voice to yell back at me, *there's no escape for you, kid!*

No signs of scary monsters. Only the forest. I turned and looked all around me. I didn't see anything unusual. Just nature. So, after my heart stopped pounding and slowed down, I took in a deep breath and continued to walk.

But that didn't last too long. Before I knew it, I had to make a sudden stop, raised my hand to my mouth as I saw her figure poking through the crowd of trees. I stared and blinked several times to make sure it wasn't just other kids from school messing around.

There, before my eyes, were flickering candles surrounding Cassandra. She raised her arms high and wide apart, making her witch's cloak look like a bird with an eight-foot wingspan. As I got closer, she seemed to be reciting an incantation as a veil of candle smoke engulfed her whole body. Suddenly, she turned to her right, grabbed a black bowl and a glass bottle, and walked over to the steaming cauldron. As she continued with her magical hymn, she gently tossed in some flour-like substance, pieces of twigs, and something resembling oil and vinegar. With a wooden stick, she stirred vigorously, creating a dense cloud of vapors.

Then out of nowhere, fairies appeared and zoomed towards her, forming a circle around her. One of them flew above her head, waving her tiny, little wand. I could see golden, glitter-like dust falling on her hair. Tinker Bell would've been proud of such a magical moment.

Quickly, the other witches joined in as they emerged from behind the trees. They tossed back their heads, arched their bodies—almost completing a circle and backward summersault while continuing to chant. Their harmonic voices raised ruckus with the animals close by. You could hear them stirring about nervously.

Were the critters afraid of something? Or was it just excitement?

I guess I was about to find out.

"Soon there will be more of us than there are of them," Cassandra sang softly.

"Whatever could she mean by that?" I whispered to myself. "More witches than regular people? Was their plan to take over the world?"

Before I knew it, a tiny fairy stood right before me and gave a dainty nod. Several nods. I guess she wanted to make sure I saw her. Then I could see about a dozen sprites, fairies, and Cassandra heading my way. The winged creatures reached me before she did and had me surrounded. My head began to spin and I was starting to experience a major freak-out! What were they going to do to me? Force me to drink some nasty witch's brew? Or turn me into the proverbial frog?

I wanted to escape, but their energy seemed to be swallowing me in like a black hole. It rendered me powerless and weak when these supernatural beings started closing in on me. All I could do was murmur: "Please don't harm me… I didn't mean to…"

Silence.

Suddenly, there she was, standing right before me with her hands behind her back…like a parent getting ready to scold a kid. She looked more regal and majestic up close than at a distance. Then slowly, she brought her right hand forward—it was holding the book. Now, with both hands, she gently started raising it over my head.

But wait, it got even scarier! The other witches had now joined her, too. It almost seemed as though the three were acting as one. They also raised up their arms, holding in their hands their ritual cup called the chalice, as they continued to chant in what sounded like Latin.

And in no time, they were all gently floating and flying around. The closer they got to me, the stronger I felt their vibes and energy. Then I realized, to my horror, that the more they formed a tight circle around me, the more powerless I became. That's when I lost it! I dropped to the ground and rolled myself into a ball, holding out the palms of my hand to shield myself.

"Stop!" I yelled. "Please don't hurt me…don't turn me into something hideous and repulsive…I'm really sorry!"

"Sometimes what people see as evil is simply fear of all that is different and unknown," Sharona Herran, one of the witches, said in a serious voice.

"It teaches us that everything you do will return three times stronger—good or bad," Cassandra interjected. "The craft of the modern-day witch is no joke."

"So, you won't be exposing me to any kind of harm—turning me into something slimy?" I started, pouting.

"No way, girl. We like you just the way you are," Cassandra chuckled sarcastically.

"Nasty and harmful spells tend to backfire on the people who cast them," another witch, Edwina Chue, cautioned.

"For real?" I humbly asked.

"Dina, no one should get carried away with spells," Cassandra warned. "Sometimes they work in unexpected ways: Results are delayed, there can be interesting side effects, they can make situations more complicated." She scratched her head with her long, black nails. "Sometimes, Dina, they just don't work."

"You know, three hundred years ago they would have hanged, beheaded, and drowned you guys," I said, joking.

"Three hundred years ago, we wouldn't have shared so much witchcraft information with any random person walking through the woods or forest," she chuckled.

"But, you know, now in modern times, they say, there's a little witch in all of us," Sharona giggled. "That's why you've been so curious about us and our special talent—and why you're here, right now."

I suddenly remembered the day I pestered them in the cafeteria, invading their space, desperately trying to get their attention. Then I immediately bowed my head, feeling the colors of embarrassment gushing to my face.

And before I knew it, they were grabbing me by my hands and walking me back to their witches' altar. Quickly, they continued with their ceremony:

"Trouble, trouble, let the cauldron bubble. Fairies, Spirits, and Sprites Hear our intentions, our wishes as you guide us through the light. As our wishes all come true, let us celebrate with delight.

Let each day be great and bright. "

After the girls finished chanting together, they wrote their own personal wishes on a small piece of paper, threw them into the cauldron, and chanted quietly to themselves. Cassandra then stirred the cast iron pot, also chanting to herself.

Then a puffy cloud of gray smoke shot upward from the cauldron! Cassandra showed-off how much more superior her powers were than the rest of them.

She proudly displayed her supernatural abilities by spinning around like a gold-medal figure skater. There she was suspended in midair, looking almost angelic, as tiny fairies sang, held hands, and frolicked all around her. I couldn't wait to tell someone—tell anyone—what I had just witnessed.

I could see her silky, ballet-looking shoes as she rose from the ground. She floated about six feet up, her arms and wide flowy sleeves appeared like wings as she flapped them gently. I watched how easily she made the whole thing look, as she pointed her toes downward and then tossed her head back.

I was so stunned I couldn't move.

Then as soft as a down feather, she returned to the ground, landing perfectly.

The other witches held hands and chanted the whole time.

Their show put a smile on my face. That could be me someday, I thought.

I realized that this was some serious stuff going on here. This was the world of the occult. I would never, ever deny its existence or joke about it again.

Too bad Gordon wasn't with me.

Still, I shivered at the thought of entering their world of powerful magic...becoming one of them. "Duh, how could I not want to be like them? Learning their craft would finally free me from being bullied. I would finally have justice—REVENGE!"

Then the girls suddenly stopped their award-winning performance.

"You know, this book of spells has been in my family for generations," Cassandra proudly admitted.

"Seriously?" I swallowed hard.

When I saw her holding up the spell book, it just sent an ice-cold shudder down my spine.

"We'd like you to take it home with you, so you can get familiar with it," Edwina interjected. "And we're hoping you can learn to respect its powerful words."

Silence.

My whole body went numb and I could feel every single hair on my skin start to rise one-by-one. I couldn't speak but did manage to crack a crooked smile.

"But the book should not be loaned to anyone else—especially someone who does not believe in the craft," Cassandra spoke in a stern voice. "You see, there could be consequences to pay."

"We're entrusting our most valued possession to you—and only you—because we've seen that you've gone through great lengths to learn more about us and what we do," they said in unison.

"But please, do handle it with care," Sharona implored, creasing her eyebrows at me. "Its contents are invaluable to us."

I nodded my head and gently placed the book in my backpack. I thanked them and quietly walked away. Too afraid to even breathe normally…as if I were carrying a priceless work of art from a museum.

But then a question suddenly popped into my head: "Can witches control the weather?" I turned around and hollered. "Make it snow, strong winds, thunder and lightning?"

"Yes, it is possible to manipulate the weather every now and then," Cassandra replied. "But only in case of emergency. So, please don't get any ideas."

10

Well, it was no secret that I was tired of feeling like an outsider, especially around the mean girls. I thought I'd look up a simple, popularity spell— one that would provide me with the confidence to show others my true colors…putting emphasis on the good, unique quality I possess.

"Alright, here goes," I rubbed my hands together, took a deep breath, and in a soft and mellow voice, I began to read the section on how to become popular. I was so anxious, I picked the first spell I saw:

"People are just drawn to me, day in and day out. I'll be forever popular without a doubt. Everyone is interested in what I say and do. Bringing me strength and confidence, that this is always true.

This great change in me, I now wish upon a star. Knowing the results, won't be very far."

Closing the book of magic, I cleared my throat and took a step back. Then I threw myself on my bed. "In the meantime, what? Just wait and see what happens at school tomorrow, I guess."

I turned off my light to gaze at my plastic, 3-D glow-the-dark stickers, scattered all over my room. They always relaxed me.

But that didn't last too long. Seconds later, I let out a chilling scream: "Noooooooo!"

The fluorescent, star-shaped stickers on my ceiling were dropping down like meteors and hitting me hard—painfully hard. Even the ones on my walls were coming at me. They were flying diagonally and almost crippling me from all sides.

I jumped to my feet because there were more stars headed my way, extra ones that weren't even put up by me.

"What the—"

Shocked, I ran and hid in my closet.

"But—but where were those extra ones coming from?" I stammered. "What went wrong? It was if they were suddenly possessed or something!"

Then it was clear to me that my first attempt at witchcraft turned out to be a huge FAIL.

But I couldn't fail, not if I wanted to become popular and get the mean girls off my back. I just couldn't. I knew I needed to consult with Cassandra right away.

So, for now, all I could do was wait. Watch. Peek to see if the effects of my botched spell were wearing-off yet.

For a second, I thought the whole experience could be funny if it weren't so scary. Ha. Anyway, once the meteor shower in my room subsided, I bolted out of my closet, grabbed my pillow and bedspread, and darted back into the closet. There was no way I would be sleeping that night. There was just no way.

The following morning, I jolted out of my closet, trying to twist and rub the soreness out of my neck. I felt like I had aged ten years overnight. When I looked in the mirror, I was startled at what I saw: My hair was bunched-up to one side, there were darks circles under my eyes—I was haggard-looking—more like a 30-year-old.

It was hard to imagine not being able to sleep in my bed tonight. Last night's event was just too disturbing for it to repeat itself again.

Later that day, I caught up with Cassandra in the cafeteria. "Listen, if I tell you about something inexplicable that happened to me last night, do you promise not to laugh or make fun of me?"

"Don't worry, I won't judge you, especially if it's spell-related," she promised.

"Wow, how did you know?"

"Oh, I had a hunch," she smiled.

"Well, anyway, it's kind of a long story," I said with a yawn.

"Tell you what," she interrupted, "just be at the forest today after school. Edwina Chue will be there to help you with your mishap and any other questions you may have."

I heaved a great big sigh and went back to sit at my table.

"Witch, witch, you're a witch. May the broom you fly crash down a ditch," Danielle and friends giggled as I passed by with my food tray.

It was obvious they had seen me talking to Cassandra and were now assuming that I was one of them, too— a witch. Good. This could help me.

I turned to them and gave them an intense, laser stare. The kind I gave my cat when she was being naughty. Well, it seemed to have had a weird effect on them. They quickly looked away and started stuffing spoons full of melon into their mouths. Even after the rotten night I had, that made my day. My week. My month!

Later that day, as soon as I entered the forest, I could feel a strong energy…powerful enough to pull me and throw my equilibrium off. It was bound to turn me into a silly klutz again.

Almost immediately, I found myself in an unusual, dark spot. My hands were reaching instinctively for tree branches and any kind of protruding shrubbery, hoping not to trip, break an ankle, or land flat on my face—like I almost did last time.

Ooooops! Too late. I knew it.

There was a thump as I hit the ground, followed by some curse words I mumbled to myself, trying to get up.

With my hands still outstretched, I managed to guide myself back to a path of a cloudless, blue sky.

When I reached a clearing in the forest, there, standing in the middle, was Edwina. As she lifted her hand gracefully into the air, a fairy and a sprite flew right to her and sat on her palm.

Then I slowly emerged from behind an enormous, fallen tree trunk and walked towards her. Without hesitation, I started telling her everything about my wacky experience the night before. I even chanted the spell for her. And again, things started falling from above. This time, it was small tree branches and leaves. They didn't hurt us, but it was annoying.

She stood there, silently staring at me.

"Are you kidding me? It's evident you didn't take your time to see if you needed to gather any ingredients for a potion!" she cried. "Your chant sounded weak and pathetic—like an alley cat, losing a fighting battle with the neighborhood dogs. Your whole technique was simply atrocious."

I suppose I could've become manic on her, but I lowered my head and covered my face with both hands instead. Then I looked at her with the respect of someone who was about to walk down the same magical path as she had, not too long ago.

"Sometimes it's tiring training new witches," Edwina admitted. "But it's what I must do to become a high-ranking witch someday."

"OMG, I'm so stupid!" I sobbed.

"You get no argument from me," she said, shaking her head.

"So, help me, please! How do I fix it?"

She took a deep breath and rolled her eyes. "One of the most common reasons newbies' spells backfire is because they are so focused on not messing-up badly that they lose their focus on what they are doing."

"But—but I read it correctly," I stammered. "The same way I read my cereal box when I'm having breakfast in the morning."

"What?" she asked, arching her eyebrows. "Seriously? Have you not heard a word I said?'

"Maybe I should've memorized it instead?" I mumbled to myself.

"Dina. Listen to me," she warned as she placed her hand on her forehead. "You have to remember that when you work with magic; you must believe that it will work. The tiniest bit of doubt will cause you to fail—or, create unpleasant results."

Pause.

"I guess I shouldn't have been so desperate, impatient, and ventured out on my own the way I did, ha? I should've just allowed you guys to train me right from the start, ha?"

Edwina nodded yes. "But, hey, don't feel too bad. Absolute belief and focus are rare in novices anyway."

"There's still hope for me, then?" My eyes widened.

"Sure. Just rehearse, rehearse, rehearse," she said, sounding more encouraging this time. "Make sure you gather any ingredients, should the spell require them, and focus on the forethought to gain the outcome you're wishing for."

"Yes. I will. I will!" I replied enthusiastically.

"And please, be aware of your energy and how you process it—it must be good to receive good in return," she cautioned.

I was now more obsessed with what other spells could be in the book. I knew I had to be careful with them or they could work against me. But the thought of possessing such power began to consume me. It was always in my brain, affecting my behavior—my personality!

11

After I got home, Gordon stopped over the house and we snacked on some fruit. "So, I guess this means you haven't giving up on the world of magic, ha?" he asked.

"Listen, I used to be stressed-out, unhappy, and frankly, dying to transfer out of this school. But now, I'm—"then I pulled out my book of spells from my backpack "—about to be very content," I finished. We both took a bite of our Granny Smith green apples.

"I finally decided to get rid of her...them."

"What?" Gordon's eyes almost popped out of their sockets.

"Figurative, that is," I grinned. "You know, ruin her popularity and mean girl status at school."

"Don't let your vendetta make you crazy!" he warned. "Keep in mind of the law of *do unto others*. You don't want to let out an awful beast...one that will capture your spirit for all eternity."

"Must you be so dramatic?" I retorted. "Give me some credit for having some self-control."

"Wow, remember, not too long ago, when you thought that witchcraft was a ruse," Gordon reiterated to me. "You said the witches preyed on the gullibility of others just to be popular and feared."

"True. All true," I admitted. "But now I know better—I was wrong about them and their craft."

Still, deep inside, I knew a big part of me just wanted revenge. By now, I was just too enraged at the mean girls. It was as though all the anger, humiliation, and embarrassment had finally exploded inside of me, leaving me numb and heartless. I couldn't ignore the strong urge to get even with them. It was a powerful feeling that kept flowing through me 24 hours a day.

"Hey, are you listening to me? I could barely hear Gordon saying. "Don't even consider some plan of evil attack as your next move, okay?" Gordon cautioned. "Just be cool."

"Yes, of course," I nodded, "I'll only use the spells for good, only for good."

"Good. Just look for a spell that will get them off your back in a subtle and kind way," he advised.

The next day was Saturday. I paced anxiously in my bedroom as the mysterious, powerful spell book laid on my bed. After one hour of hesitating to even touch it, I closed my eyes and began to open it excruciatingly slow… as if fearing malicious entities would escape and come after me. It even made the unnerving, creaking sound, like the proverbial, old coffin being opened by its vampire.

I Suddenly, I felt strange and off-balance. There was a strong pull of energy coming from the book.

Something was drawing me to it like a powerful magnet. It was getting harder to ignore and resist it. *Dina...Dina...* I could almost swear it was speaking to me. As if this ancient book was calling my name and wanted me to be its new owner and reader...wanted me to read all its pages...study it and learn all about it. Then it happened—*I OPENED IT!*

Immediatcly I was desperately flipping through its pages, hoping to find something intense and effective... something to save and rescue me...something stronger and more powerful than the popularity spell. Then, when I was ready to give up, there it was, in black, bold letters:

Defend Yourself and Fight Back Now Spell

It was the section in the book on how to retaliate against anyone or anything. This was the section that contained the spells on how to get even...punch back... teach them a lesson. But could it work for someone who had already botched a spell before?

Probably—but not right away. Edwina did say that I had to practice on focusing.

Heck, I'm sure even Cassandra and her coven of witches weren't born with their powers, weren't chanting spells, and mixing potions while still in diapers, weren't worthy of wearing gothic medieval robes and cloaks in pre-school either.

Well, as I felt less discouraged, I continued to search for the perfect spell. When I got to the middle, I started shaking with excitement, and a bit of fear, too. I found myself fixated on the most enchanting group of words I had ever seen:

Be Mean to Me No More

Finally, the perfect title, followed by the perfect spell for me—and hopefully awesome results — appeared.

My confidence was soaring and I was feeling powerful — as if I'd been brave and daring all my life.

This was the new and better me. No one would ever dare humiliate me again. But even if they tried, HELLO, SPELL BOOK, my new BFF. Chant. Chant. Chant. With one spell, my life could change forever.

I could, after all, be leaving a life of misery, with the ability to get even with back-stabbers, mean girl-clicks, immature and silly boys, too...the list would be endless.

I convinced myself I was making the right decision. I could soon have power over these people. Then it hit me. Wow, I wouldn't even have to study long hours for tests at school anymore—I could cast a spell to have built-in knowledge. And more importantly, I would never have to worry about anything for the rest of my life.

12

Then it happened…a sign that life would only get better. The following day at school, as the three of them walked in unison towards their lockers—like they were conjoined triplets, I put into action my best ninja moves ever by quietly walking behind them. I started mumbling to myself the special spell I found for them:

> "Because to me, you've been so mean
> you now will bow to me, down on your knees.
> Your mouths will hurt, while they burst with jelly beans.
> The thought of me will haunt you with great fear whether I'm far, whether I'm near.
> Forever paralyzed with fright you shall remain by day and by night."

Instantaneously, their cheeks looked like they were packed with small marbles—or like a hamster storing food. They couldn't speak because their cheeks were filled with jelly beans. The girls were having trouble spiting them out, chewing, and swallowing them, too.

Right away, the smell of sweet candy permeated the hall. And before I knew it, they were falling to their knees, tightening their eyes, clasping their hands tightly around my ankles, and begging for mercy—through grunts and groans, of course. It was AWESOME!

Then I turned to my right and saw two eighth-grade boys with their mouths wide open, bumping their skinny knuckles together. The bell rang.

The on-lookers around us who were also shocked and speechless, started scrambling to their classes. The girls' squinting eyes widened as the jelly beans were beginning to dissolve in their mouths. Simultaneously, they swallowed what was now fruit juice. Maya and Gina released their buckled hands around my feet and bolted out of there.

"Maybe that'll teach you to never mess with me again!" I shouted as I gulped hard.

"I didn't mean it," Danielle wailed, backing away from me in the direction of the stairways behind her. When she reached the stairs, she took a little stumble and dip, but then quickly recovered her balance. Suddenly, she started blinking uncontrollably and making bizarre facial expressions like some actor in a silent film before making a mad dash down the stairs.

I almost felt sorry for Danielle. Almost.

"Excellent touch, Dina," Gordon said in a disappointed tone. He turned the corner and left.

Then one last ripple of brazenness hit me. I straightened my posture, brushed my hair, and went to my next class… trying to convince myself that what I had just done wasn't so bad… that any karma headed my way, because of this action, shouldn't be too bad.

When I walked into my class, I could feel the stares of everyone. Then they all flashed me a quick smile and immediately turned away. What I had been waiting for my whole life had now come true—people were finally going to look at me with respect!

After class, I could feel all eyes on me as I walked through the halls. Part of me felt like a celebrity while the other part felt like I was a specimen under glass, being studied.

After I got home, I was relieved that I didn't lose my cool casting the spell. But at the same time, there was now an unexplained new layer of fear that was beginning to emerge deep inside of me.

Shortly after, Gordon came over the house.

"But why are you so upset with me?" I wailed. "I thought you'd be pleased by my act of bravery…me, finally standing-up for myself."

"Listen, I understand it was pent-up, accumulative anger that finally made you blow-up," Gordon said, sounding more like a parent than a kid. "But you didn't use the right spell, Dina. And you'll have to pay for it later—one way or another."

"You think the girls' parents and everyone in town will come after me? Try to get rid of me…run me and my family out of town…ostracize me? Or something worse like…"

"Oh, stop being such a drama queen," Gordon interrupted. "The town's people won't be coming after you with torches and stones. All that can happen is that the school will expel you. You'll just have to move to another school, after all."

I raised my eyebrows and choked. "Wow, that's really comforting. Thanks, friend."

"Listen, it's a far better scenario than being drowned and burned at the stake like at the Salem witch trials of 1692," Gordon tilted his head to one side. "Which by the way, they were only hanged, and they weren't even witches, either."

"But I don't want to be expelled—I'll be so grounded—you've got to help me," I cried. "You always have a sensible answer to everything. "

He shook his head. "Dina, I really doubt Danielle and the girls will rat on you anyway."

"How do you know that?"

"Well, for starters, they'd be afraid to speak-up because they've been mean to so many kids at school themselves," he assured me. "Some of those kids could take your side and finally retaliate against them. It would eventually be the school against them.

"So, karma is all I have to worry about?"

"But that can be just as bad as what you did to them."

"But it'll be a one-time thing, and I won't ever have to worry about it ever again!"

"Maybe. Maybe not. I don't know—only the UNIVERSE does!"

For the next several days, the mean girls were quiet and kept to themselves. There was also a change in the air and the energy around the school. But even stranger than that, I found myself suddenly popular. Yes. That's right. *Popular.* Schoolmates who once ignored me and made me feel invisible were now waving at me, "Hey, Dina. What's up?"

At lunch time, I took a deep breath as I looked forward to enjoying my meal without any bullies lurking around. I dropped my lunch tray on the table and took my seat. "I'm really starting to like this school now," I confessed to Gordon. "This year is going to be a great year after all."

Then I opened my milk carton and took a long, big gulp. When I put it down, Gordon stared at me in horror — gawked at me in disbelief.

"What? What's wrong?" I asked, annoyed. "Do I have a milk mustache or something?"

"It's a mustache alright," he said, cringing. "But it's not a white one—it's forest green."

"Huh? Shut up, liar!" I shouted. "Seriously. Quit messing with me."

"Look for yourself," Gordon handed me a napkin.

I wiped my upper lip and then looked inside my milk carton. Both were green. Dark green.

"Yuck! It must be spoiled!" I shrieked, slapping it off the table with the back of my hand.

"Mine isn't," Gordon assured me.

Other kids nearby looked at their milk and shrugged, indicating that theirs looked fine, too.

"Ooh, what the heck is going on here?" I felt panic starting to take over me.

"Eek!" Gordon shrilled. "Your skin. It's turning purple. Your tongue...bright orange."

Other students who were witnessing this phenomenon nodded in agreement.

I stood up, turned my back on Gordon and raised my clenched fists in the air. I could feel my blood surging through my body like a cauldron of rage. In no time, I was starting to feel the color of embarrassment spreading all over my face. Part of me wished I was invisible, but most of me just wanted to die.

At a distance, about four rows of tables away, was Cassandra and the girls. I could see their drab look of disappointment on their faces as they quietly ate their lunch. I had let them down once again.

"Dina!" Gordon hollered.

But all I wanted to do was camouflage myself into the walls, so I hurried along and ignored him. As I ran to the girl's bathroom—again, I could hear kids and their random opinions about what had just happened to me.

"She looks like a blueberry. I think she might be contagious."

And "Dude, that's some intense smell of jelly beans. Is that coming from her?"

And "Wholly— Her tongue is like an orange Starburst candy!"

And "That girl has been slowly mutating into some major FREAK-O lately."

And "Look at her. What's wrong with her??"

I tried scrubbing the color off my skin and tongue with wet paper towels, but it was useless. I shook my head, puzzled. Clearly, there was something afoot here. Was this karma coming back to bite me? I thought.

Eventually, the colors started to gradually disappear on their own. I had a couple of minutes to spare before the late bell for my next class, so I darted out of there.

Then as I dashed through the halls, I caught Gordon's head protruding out of his classroom door as if he was looking for me. "I told you something was bound to happen to you," he chastised me. "I told you and I told you and…"

"Fine, fine," I interrupted him, throwing my hands up in defeat. "You were right. You're always right about these things, okay?"

13

I wish I could say that my predicament had ended, but it continued for a whole week. Sometimes the bright, fruity colors would hit me, embarrassing me to death while walking in the halls, sometimes in the library, and once, while walking to school. I arrived one day at the campus looking like a rainbow.

And then on the seventh day of my karmic ordeal, the universe showed me a sign … a hint that it might be starting to be more lenient with me. It appeared that my punishment for my vengeful ways was starting to diminish. But still, that day didn't end without something weird happening to me.

On that day, my body and tongue did not go through the chameleon-color change. So naturally, I thought I was done paying for all harm I caused the girls. But after my last class ended, when I arrived at my locker and opened it, I felt my throat tighten as I took several steps back. The jelly bean curse was not done with me yet. The candy started gushing out and hitting the floor, like torrential rains during a stormy season.

Some students, who apparently weren't fazed by this occurrence, started picking and eating the ones from the top of the heap.

"Hey! I get it now," one kid said. "This whole jelly bean thing has been like a pre-Halloween stunt, ha?"

I raised my eyebrows, smiled but remained speechless, too mortified to speak.

"Nah, I think it's all magic," a girl next to him said. "She's friends with those witches, you know."

"Pretty cool, whatever it is," he chuckled as he popped the candy into his mouth.

"It's best to stay away from her," said a girl, poking her head through the crowd, "before you, too, are lured to the world of the occult."

"Yeah," her friend interjected, "they say that once you venture into that world, it will eventually have a negative effect on you!"

Meanwhile, Gordon stood several lockers away, looking clearly astounded as he mouthed *wow* to me.

Later that day, while still working on my homework, there was a thump at my window. It sounded like a bird hurrying to safety before the sun went down. But when I looked up, I was alarmed to see a questionable silhouette behind my flowing curtains. I was sure I saw a head, just couldn't tell if it was human or animal.

Had Gordon returned to play a joke on me? Was it a raccoon? The neighbor's pet chimp?

I sprinted to my window. No ladder was anywhere nearby, so it couldn't have been Gordon. Besides, he wasn't strong or big enough to carry such a big thing. Dumb. Then I stuck my head way out to see if it might be an animal. Nothing. Whatever it was either fell to the ground or swiftly and skillfully climbed back down. Hmmm.

But just as I started closing my window, some animal or someone appeared to be messing with our garden gnomes. I was sure that it was the animal whose head I saw. So, I soared outside to catch the critter in the act before the sun went down.

There I stood in the middle of the lawn, with very little sunlight left, shooing away whatever it was that I saw.

"Oooooh," I panicked as I hit the lawn. Kicking and waving my arms around like a maniac, I jolted back onto my feet. Then I felt something wrapping around my ankles. I thought for sure the fairies had returned to torment me again.

But as I looked down below, I screamed at the top of my lungs. "Oh, no!" And before I could blink, I was knocked down to the ground again; my sneakers and one sock were pulled off and went flying over my head.

I was even more alarmed when I saw the creepiest little pudgy hands blocking most of my blood circulation to my toes with their death grip. I couldn't believe what I was seeing. The freaky, stubby hands were attached to a couple of the most wicked, hideous-looking garden gnomes—right from our very own back yard!

I lay there, no longer able to move from the horror of what I was witnessing. "Hey—let me go!" I wailed. "Let go of me!"

Then my screaming turned to sobbing as the vicious little trolls were now dragging me across the lawn.

And just when I thought my nightmare couldn't get any worse, I raised my head and could now see dark figures poking out from our bushes and shrubs, all along our back wall. There was now an army of them. They started multiplying like crazy. I could see their little, stumpy shapes all over the place. They seemed to be in a hurry, scrambling from one corner of our yard to another.

"What—what do you want from me?!"

Desperately, I tried grabbing at the freshly cut grass, but it was too short. It was like trying to clutch onto the carpet fibers.

The nasty gremlins now had me surrounded, tugging and pulling me closer and closer into a very dark hole. A hole I had never seen before — a very deep and scary hole.

Where were they taking me?
Would I become one of them?
Would this be the end of me?

For a moment there, I felt like I could break away and overpower them—but I was wrong. Through my peripheral vision, I saw one of the gnomes reaching into his pant pocket, clutched tightly to something, and then rudely dumped it all over my face. I was not only sneezing this time, but I started feeling drowsy and coughing uncontrollably.

Seconds later, all I could do was let out a weak and faint gasp. Like a rag doll, I lay flat on my back. My rickety legs were now halfway in the hole. I had no strength left in me and could no longer move a finger.

Then as they flipped me over on my stomach to push me in easier, I saw our backyard light suddenly turned on. I thought I heard some footsteps, but I couldn't see anyone. But something even better happened.

"Dina!" Dad called. Are you out here?"

The gnomes quickly vanished—literately into the night. I was finally able to break away from the powerful, ominous hex they seemed to have put on me. I stood up feeling normal, wiping the dirt off my pants.

"Yep, I'm right back here, Dad."

"Dina, you're not wearing shoes and you're missing a sock," he said, raising his eyebrows, looking perplexed.

"Ah, well, you see…"

"Oh, wait," Dad interrupted as he pointed. "Isn't that them over by the pergola?"

"There they are!" I let out a big sigh and loped to get them.

Mom opened the back door. "What's all the commotion back here?"

"I thought I saw a racoon," I replied.

"That's Nuts! It could've had rabies!" she wailed.

"So why were your shoes off?" Dad sounded curious.

"Well, you didn't let me finish," I chuckled. "I removed them, so I could be quieter when sneaking up on it."

"Kid, you really worry me sometimes," he nodded his head. "Please stay away from the wildlife."

I gave them both a nervous, half smile as we all went back inside.

I was too shaky still to text or call Gordon about the gnomes that night and went straight to bed.

But later that night, I was having a hard time staying focused on, well, everything. It was after midnight before I started dozing off. I guess I had it coming to me.

14

The next morning was one of those difficult ones; I couldn't get out of bed. After a bizarre and torturous experience with the haunted gnomes, followed by relentless, lucid nightmares all night long, I wasn't well rested and ready to face the world yet. But my mother's voice, getting closer and closer to my room, was telling me I better be ready.

"Dina!" she called, knocking repetitiously on my door. "There's something I have to show you. Now."

Rubbing my eyes, I dragged myself across my floor and lethargically opened my door. My mother burst in, wearing her weekend gardening attire: wide-rim hat, garden gloves, long-sleeve cotton blouse.

"Hey, what's the big deal?" I grumbled.

"What—what is the meaning of this?" she stammered.

"It's your plant equipment, carryall thing," I said between yawns. "Without the equipment, I guess."

"Well, didn't you take them last night?" she quavered. "I just saw them all scattered under the bushes, by the back wall."

I flatly and emphatically denied it. "That's crazy, Mom! What would I want with your pruning shears, shovels, or claw rakes?"

"But you were there last night!" she said with a scolding look on her face. "And there appears to be a hole that was dug up and refilled again."

"What? How?"

She crossed her arms in frustration then pointed to our backyard.

Immediately it hit me. Those despicable beings borrowed her stuff and dug that hole. The hole I almost went into.

I bolted out of my room and let out a scream that echoed throughout the whole house. When I got to the backyard, my eyes bulged as I let out a faint gasp. There they were, spread out under the bushes, around the covered hole — Mom's outdoor utensils. The creepy gnomes, standing in their usual spots, were only a few feet away. I walked towards them and stared at them coldly. They stared back…their eyes following me like the eyes of a spook portrait on a wall.

Then I ran back inside the house wailing like a baby, confessing to Mom that I was guilty. It was so much easier than telling her the horrifying truth—a lot more credible too.

"Dina," she said in a disappointing tone. "That's all you had to do. Tell the truth. Just tell the truth."

"Hahahahaha!" Gordon cracked up almost convulsing. "You know, there are books and movies about those stocky guys."

"Please, give me a break. I've just been through a harrowing experience!"

"Sorry," Gordon said, clearing his throat.

"This was for real. This really happened. They almost kidnapped me and…"

"Okay, all joking aside, Dina, those short but muscular characters have a reputation of being malicious clowns and obnoxious jokesters—you know, like when they come to life."

"But they've been in the family for three generations—without any problems." I professed.

"Just as I suspected," Gordon's smile faded. "This is your fault…you, and only you, are to blame for opening these floodgates to the world of the unknown…the world of the supernatural."

"But I never cast a spell on them!"

"You didn't have to. All you had to do was mess around with magic and witchcraft, not follow the rules, or not know what you were doing—and viola! You opened-up a portal of negativity.

"Well, how can I close it up again?" I wailed.

"What parallel, alternate universe do you reside in?" Gordon bellowed. "Get out of that bubble, where you think you can patch-up everything in life like baby boo-boos, with just a band-aid. "

My body went numb.

"You have to understand, Dina, sometimes when rookies like you mess with witchcraft, or even the *Ouija Board,* it can invite unknown consequences!"

"Okay, I get how karma works, but how are these portals connected to my magic mishap?"

"Well, they're supposed to be a link or doorway between our physical world and the spirit world," Gordon spoke in a serious tone. "Spirits are able to enter our world through these openings."

"Oh no," I muttered. "I am now living in bizarro world."

"I'm sorry, but fiddling with rituals can create these glitches," he stressed. "You're going to need a cleansing—you know, sage, white candles, holy water, crystals and salt."

"Huh?" I shook my head. "Like they do for haunted houses?"

"Yes. But no worries, I'll help you gather the ingredients when you're ready."

Great. Now I would have to worry about getting my parents out of the house, so I could walk around cleansing myself and our home. I mean, how else would I be able to go from room to room, deflecting and clearing them of negative energies? Not with parents there, that's for sure.

"Oh, and Dina, don't wait too long to cleanse the house," he warned, "because if you do, the list of terrifying happenings will only get longer."

15

After school, as I walked by Mrs. Foster's classroom, I let out a frightening gasp. Standing right in front of her door's narrow window, was ghost girl. I mean, I could really see her. She was looking quite ghastly and deathly, like any ghoul would, I suppose. But just knowing that she was a mere child like me when she passed put me in a deeper state of melancholy.

Obviously shaken by what I had just witnessed, I could almost feel every one of my teeth dissolving from their heavy shattering.

When she gazed right at me, she appeared hungry to communicate something about herself. But something was holding her back. Whatever that was, made her look up, shake her head, and fill her face with shame. It was as if something or someone was telling her not to speak.

But what really defined her face were her eyes. They looked disappointed, sad, and extraordinarily despondent. And even though her look was peaceful, it also appeared strong-willed and anxious, too. I suddenly felt this whole experience fascinating and riveting.

Was she regretting her once practical jokester way of life here on earth? Could she be yearning to finally move on with her afterlife? Who knows? She still wasn't speaking.

It occurred to me that maybe the people from Lingering Souls, aka Ghost Catchers, could probably help her move on to the other side.

Well, anyway, when I raised my quivering hand to wave good-bye to her, she gently turned her head to one side and started spinning around again. Then suddenly she vanished. Poof—gone. Back into the darkness of the other dimension.

I was really starting to lose it. The non-stop series of supernatural events was starting to make me feel whacky, insane, and nutzoid—like I should be locked-up and committed. I couldn't find a spell in the book to counteract the mess I was now in, either. Well, I could no longer just stand by and let this crisis crush me. So, I bolted out of there for an emergency consultation with my favorite witches.

"Don't you see what you've done? You've set this whole nightmare in motion!!" Edwina Rocha gasped. "It's usually what happens when newbies become dangerously curious."

"I get that I did a very stupid thing—I have a friend that keeps reminding me of that," I wailed. "But I was so consumed with anger and vengeance that…"

"Sure, I understand, but you still broke the laws of magic, Dina," she said, putting her hands on her hips.

I put my head down, struggling to hold back my emotions. Not to cry. Not to have a meltdown.

"The assumption was that you were going to follow directions, either by practicing magic correctly with us, or by carefully reading the warnings in the book!" Cassandra snapped.

"It's just that when I got to the section on revenge, I found its strange force irresistible," I confessed.

"You know, Dina, when we loaned you the book, we were testing you," Edwina admitted.

"You were?" I looked at her with sad, puppy eyes — like a puppy after he's had an accident on the floor.

"Sure. We needed to see how disciplined you would be. How focused and serious you would feel about the world of magic."

"Obviously, you've had a rough start—especially since you used it for revenge," Sharona interjected. "We can no longer trust you with our ancient, priceless book."

"But don't feel bad, you can continue your training with us," Cassandra said, now sounding more mellow. "Only then will you be well-versed and develop more self-control."

"So, no more spell book?" I asked disappointedly.

Edwina shook her head. "Well, not ours, that's for sure. But if you really must have one now, you can purchase one for beginners online."

"Online? No—please." I begged. "I need your book…I have to find a powerful counter spell!"

"There are no spells for your situation, Dina," Cassandra declared. "What's happening to you now is your karmic debt. You must let it take its course… even your friend has told you that."

"But what do I do to lessen the severity of my karma, now?"

"Absolutely nothing," Edwina professed. "Just deal with it until it passes—and hopefully you'll learn from it."

"Of course," I frowned. "Deep inside, I knew there was no way out of this situation. I guess I just needed to hear it from you guys."

"Don't freak out, kid," Sharona professed, crossing her arms in front of her. "You can work on your weaknesses with a simpler book for now."

"Of course, why didn't I think of that," I mumbled to myself. "I'll show them just how serious I am about magic."

Then as I attempted to make a mad dash out of there, Cassandra grabbed my shoulder and pulled me back. "Hold on a second, Dina."

Oh no, more scolding I thought. But when I turned to look at her, she handed me a single stem of a yellow snapdragon flower. "Are you familiar with these?" she asked.

"Yep, I sure am. My mother grows a bunch of these in her garden."

"Good," she smiled. "They could come in handy someday."

"Handy? How?"

"Well, let me explain," she kneeled on the damp ground and pulled me down with her. "Ancient culture once thought the flower's seeds had supernatural powers."

"What?"

"Yes. The tiny skull-looking pods were believed to protect against sorcery, witchcraft, and curses."

"OMG!" I shrieked in disbelief. "I have to admit the dried-up shells are pretty creepy-looking."

"All through history, people have always thought that they resemble human heads," Cassandra added.

"Hmmmm, I think they're more alien looking," I retorted.

"Hahahahaha," she laughed hysterically. "Oh, and by the way, it was also believed they contained anti-aging powers, too."

"Wow. Thanks for enlightening me with all these details," I told her as I caressed my face, feeling around for any premature wrinkles.

Then as I walked home, I thought, *who would ever put a spell on me? What would be the chances of that happening, anyway?* Oh well, I was far too much in a good mood to worry about what ifs. I was about to purchase my very own spell book…on my very own prepaid debit card.

Later that evening, I let my cat, Sheba, out in the garden. I noticed a red-tail hawk swooping low from the neighbor's tree to our wall. He had his eye on my kitty.

"Stay away you beast!" I commanded." I won't let you fly off with my pet—evil predator!"

The hawk flew away several houses down the street. Then I got an eerie feeling the bird could have been sent by one of the witches…secretly following me… watching and snooping on me. I remembered reading about animal guides in the spell book. They also called them *familiars,* whose main purpose was to assist witches.

Gordon also mentioned once that often small pets would vanish in areas where witches practiced magic. Sometimes these supernatural entities would be used for good, but other times, for bad. Could the girls be so upset with me about breaking the rules that they would send this hawk to spy on me—or worse, send the feathered carnivore to devour my Siamese cat?

Who knows?

But I wasn't taking any chances.

Then my cat looked up at me and gave me one of those soundless meows. You know, the kind when they open their mouth and you can't hear anything. I grabbed her and quickly took her back inside.

Days later, my spell book arrived in the mail. But instead of being crazy and excited when I opened it, I plopped on my bed, almost depressed. My mind was suddenly struck with warnings from Gordon and the witches: *Whatever you put out to the universe will always come back to you three-fold.* And, *the spells should never be used to control other human beings. They should only be used as teaching tools, and for helping those in need.*

I decided to wait until the following day to start reading it.

The next day was Saturday. After a quick breakfast, I dashed right back upstairs to my room. I was feeling better about the book and couldn't wait to delve into it. Then it hit me. I lacked self-control. I'd have to be nuts to lose my cool again while attempting to cast another spell. Could I handle having to deal with a second-round of karma…and possibly opening new portals to who-knows-what other menacing things?

"No way!"

I needed to get rid of the book. I couldn't return it because no refunds were allowed. So, I walked to the curbside and threw it in our trash can. The can was packed and overflowing with the cover ajar. Most of the book was protruding and exposed, but I managed to squeeze it in there, somehow.

"No more spells for me," I mumbled to myself. "I've learned my lesson well and will never mess with the supernatural again—EVER!"

When I went back to my room, I took a deep breath in, and opened my curtains to let in some sunshine. I was feeling really relieved about tossing my book out and deciding not to toy with the occult and magic anymore.

Then I almost choked. I couldn't believe what I was witnessing. Danielle was heading towards my house. In her hands, she appeared to be carrying a neatly wrapped gift, which she then placed in our mail box. I was sure it was for me, probably an apologetic gesture, making amends and a peace offering. *Sweet.* As she started walking away, the spell book dropped to the ground. She was startled and turned around to pick it up. But instead of putting it back into the trash can, she stared at the cover and frantically started skimming through the pages. Then a smile broke across her face as she clenched my book tightly against her chest and dashed away with it.

At that moment, even if I had run like a maniac and caught up to her, there was no way she would've handed it to me, anyway? NO WAY!

So, I stood there petrified, as tiny beads of perspiration started oozing out of every pour on my skin.

"Oh, no! Bubble, bubble, I'm in trouble," I howled. "Mom! Help! I think I'm going to need a dozen of your dried-up snapdragon flower seeds—FAST!

92

Turn ahead for a preview of
the next book in the bizarre
Creepified series:

"Out of Body"

1

"Aiden Campbell!" Mr. Martin Called. "Excuse me?" I said as I lifted my head off my desk, groggy, and wiping drool from my cheek.

The classroom was empty.

Mr. Martin shook his head. Then he sat at the desk right in front of me, staring icily at me. "Aiden, you're not going to like what I have to say to you."

I gulped and slowly started sinking into my desk. "This is horrible!" I shrieked. "I fell asleep again, didn't I?"

"That you did. And Aiden, I'm a bit worried," he began. "Because if you keep this up, you're going to fail my class...**ALL** of your classes."

"I understand...you— don't have to explain," I stammered. "My parents have to be notified, right?"

"It's for your own good," Mr. Martin sympathized. "Especially after I've given you so many chances already."

He then wrote a big red *I*, for incomplete, of course, on my quiz paper, and walked out quietly with his briefcase in one hand and sweater on the other. By now, the butterflies in my stomach had turned into bats as I buried my face in my hands. Walking home, I convinced myself that all I had to do was pretend that everything was cool: keep-up appearances at home until the school's office contacted my parents.

"I'm dying to know…" Mom blurted out at me as I walked in the house, "why does your principal need to speak to us next week?"

I felt the butterflies coming back. "Uh…it's…it's about important stuff," I caught myself stammering again. "So, you know already?"

Then as I turned around to grab a water bottle out of the refrigerator, I saw the printed email taped on the door. In black, bold letters it read:

To the Parents of Aiden Campbell:
It has come to our attention…

I was mortified and couldn't read the rest. "Mom, can we just drop it for now?" I begged her, "I suddenly need to lie down.

Doomsday was closer than I thought.

Well, it was Monday morning—JUDGEMENT DAY. The principal, Mr. Johnson, scheduled our appointment at 7 a.m. so I wouldn't miss my first class and my parents could arrive to work on time. Feeling quite tormented, I paused at the bottom of school stairs. A wave of angst suddenly struck me as I thought about how severe my punishment might be. What would become of me if I didn't graduate middle school with the rest of my friends?

"Aiden, don't slouch," Mom whispered. "It's not the end of the world."

Dad peeked over Mom's shoulder. "Son, straighten your collar," he said in a stern voice.

Suddenly, I could smell Mr. Johnson. Whatever those liquids or sprays were that he splashed onto himself every morning before arriving to school, they always seemed to nauseate everyone and make their heads pound. Sure enough, he walked in five minutes later. That was always the cool thing about him; his scent always warned us that he was nearby.

"Good morning, folks," he greeted politely. He put his insulated lunch bag in his top desk drawer, turned on his computer, and glared at me.

"How bad is it?' I asked naively.

"I'm sure you have an idea," he grinned as he leaned back on his leather chair. "Your test scores and grades have been slipping—you've plummeted from As and Bs to Ds since the school year started."

Both my parents gasped and clutched their chests. "What's happening to you, Aiden?" They both cried out in unison.

"His brain must be shrinking!" Dad snapped. "That's why we're here!"

"I'm so upset with you, kid, I don't know what to do with you!" Mom added, rubbing her forehead quite hard.

Could this nightmare have been any worse? I felt the walls start to close in on me, like some torture room in a cheesy, low-budget horror movie. I was sure that my life, as I knew it, would be forever disturbed. Then something scarier happened. The principal told my parents that I was failing because I was falling asleep in class, resulting in incomplete quizzes and tests. He told them that homework assignments were the only things I was completing.

"I'm sorry!" I exclaimed. "I can't go to sleep early… I'm having trouble with that…it's really bad."

"You have insomnia and never told us?" Mom pressed.

"I was hoping it would go away by now," I said calmly.

"So, it never occurred to you to drink a little warm milk? Eat some turkey or oatmeal?" Dad grumbled. "You just lay there in the dark, tossing and turning?"

"Well, no—not exactly," I replied. "I have the TV on, I'm Facebooking, texting, playing video games—"

"Hold on!" Mr. Johnson interrupted nodding his head. "Teenagers generally stay up late; they tend to be more alert in the evening. But this day and age, the stimulation of everything you just mentioned has made matters worse for many adolescents like yourself."

"So, it's not really insomnia?" I asked excitedly.

"Probably not." He said.

"You're still grounded, kid!" Mom wailed. "You will no longer be allowed to use any of your electronic devices at bedtime either."

"NO—please," I pleaded. "Not all at once."

"Listen to me, Aiden. It is important you work on relaxing and switching off all electronics at a decent time." Mr. Johnson suggested. "You have to do this or you're going to have to repeat the seventh grade."

Finally, now I had one thing I didn't have before.
Hope.

About the Author

S.L. Armend lives in Southern Arizona with her cat, Glee, and has always been a fan of fantasy, thriller, and the supernatural. She grew up watching Rod Serling's television series, The Twilight Zone, The Outer Limits, and Night Gallery. In the 1980s, she also enjoyed the series Tales from the Darkside and Tales from the Crypt. She is currently working on her new short story for her Creepified series.

Visit her online at

https://www.facebook.com/pg/CreepifiedSeries-100785261752677/posts/?ref=page_internal